Chapter One

Ursula woke up early one Saturday morning and looked at the blue summer sky.

"Who wants to come for a picnic by the river?" she said to her sixteen teddy bears.

The bears all gazed into space and said nothing. Even Fredbear, Ursula's favourite, went on staring at the wall.

"You're all a lot of lazy-bones," said Ursula. She pulled on her shorts and T-shirt and ran downstairs.

Ursula lived with her Aunt Prudence. She found her aunt in the kitchen, making pancakes for breakfast, and singing *The sun has got his hat on*, at the top of her voice.

"Hip hip hip hurray!" sang Ursula, joining in the song.

Aunt Prudence flipped the pancake over and caught it in the pan. "You sound happy today," she said.

"I am happy," said Ursula. "The sun's shining, there are pancakes for breakfast, it's Saturday and there's no school." She put her arms round her aunt's waist. "Can I have a picnic by the river, Aunt Prudence, please?"

This book is due for return on or before the last date shown below.

Don Gresswell Ltd., London, N21   Cat. No. 1207

DG 02242/71

004906

HAMISH HAMILTON LTD

Published by the Penguin Group
27 Wrights Lane, London w8 5tz, England
Viking Penguin Inc., 40 West 23rd Street, New York, New York 10010, USA
Penguin Books Australia Ltd, Ringwood, Victoria, Australia
Penguin Books Canada Ltd, 2801 John Street, Markham, Ontario, Canada l3r 1b4
Penguin Books (NZ) Ltd, 182–190 Wairau Road, Auckland 10, New Zealand

Penguin Books Ltd, Registered Offices: Harmondsworth, Middlesex, England

First published in Great Britain by Hamish Hamilton Ltd 1990

Set in 15pt Baskerville

A CIP catalogue record for this book is available from the British Library

isbn 0-241-12962-1

Typeset by Rowland Phototypesetting (London) Ltd
Printed in Great Britain at the University Press, Cambridge

"We'll see," said Aunt Prudence. "I've got a lovely surprise for you first."

Ursula sat down at the kitchen table. She knew it must be something nice by the big smile on her aunt's face.

Then Ursula noticed that four places had been laid at the table. She stared in astonishment.

"Who's coming for breakfast?" she said.

"That's the surprise," said Aunt Prudence. She tipped the pancake onto a plate and put it down in front of Ursula. "Ian and Jamie are coming for the weekend," she said.

"Oh!" said Ursula, gazing at her aunt in dismay. The weekend was

ruined. Her cousins Ian and Jamie were awful. Especially Ian, who teased her all the time and called her a baby, just because she loved dear old Fredbear with his bald tummy and his one glass eye.

Ursula didn't feel hungry any more. She scowled down at her pancake. "Why didn't you tell me before?" she said.

"Aunt Maggie only phoned last night," said Aunt Prudence. "She and Uncle Andy have to go up to town, and they're dropping the boys off on the way."

A car horn tooted outside the house. Aunt Prudence looked at the clock.

"That'll be them now," she said,

going to the door.

Ursula dashed out of the kitchen and raced upstairs. She had to hide Fredbear before that horrible Ian got his hands on him. Ian had once tied Fredbear to a stake and tried to set fire to him. She must make sure that nothing like that happened this time.

Ursula heard voices in the hall and feet on the stairs. She grabbed Fredbear, pushed him hurriedly into bed and covered him with the blankets. Then a noise behind her

made her turn round. Ian was
standing in the doorway.

"Come on, Ursula," he said.
"Let's have breakfast. Aunt
Prudence says we can go for a
picnic later on."

Had he seen, or hadn't he?

Ursula didn't know. All she could
do was keep her fingers crossed as
she followed her cousin downstairs.

Chapter Two

Ian and Jamie thought that Ursula was just an ordinary girl, but she had a secret that even Aunt Prudence didn't know about. Ursula could turn herself into a bear.

It was very simple. Ursula had found the magic spell in a book in the library. All she needed were a few magic words, and a currant bun, stuffed with a mixture of porridge oats and honey. Ursula had tried it and the spell really worked. She could turn herself into a bear whenever she liked, and a beefburger and chips turned her into a girl again every time.

Ursula found that turning into a bear could be very useful sometimes, and she always liked to have the right sort of currant bun with her everywhere she went. That was why she put one in her rucksack later that morning, before setting off for a picnic with Ian and Jamie.

"Now, have you got enough food?" said Aunt Prudence, helping them on with their rucksacks.

"I think so, thanks," grinned Ian. "Egg and tomato sandwiches, smokey bacon crisps, an apple and a carton of orange juice. Oh, yes. And

a carrot each, because it's good for our teeth."

"Hee-haw!" bellowed Jamie, galloping away down the street. Ian laughed and ran off after his brother.

Ursula stared as she watched them go. Ian's rucksack was stuffed so full it was almost bursting. It couldn't all be food. There was something else in that rucksack, and Ursula wondered what it could be . . .

She sighed and followed the two boys down the hill towards the river. She wished she didn't have to go, but soon the fresh air and the sunshine made her feel better. By the time they reached the bridge she was feeling more cheerful.

She didn't stay cheerful for long.

Ian and Jamie stopped to look down into the river, waiting for her to catch up. Ursula stood beside them on the bridge, and all three gazed down at the rushing water.

Ian took off his rucksack and unfastened the strap.

"I wonder if this stupid old teddy can swim," he said to Jamie. And out of the rucksack he pulled a very squashed-looking Fredbear.

"IAN! NO!" shouted Ursula, as he dangled Fredbear over the rail by one foot. Jamie made a grab.

"Let me do it, Ian," he said, pulling at his brother's arm. "I want to chuck him in."

Ursula watched in horror as the two boys pulled Fredbear in opposite

directions as if he were the rope in a tug-of-war. She never found out exactly how it happened, or whether they really meant to drop Fredbear off the bridge. But before she could do anything to stop them, both boys suddenly let go at the same time. Fredbear fell into the river with a splash.

"Oh dear. What a shame," said Ian.

Chapter Three

Ursula blinked back the tears as she
saw the river carry Fredbear quickly
away downstream. Crying wouldn't
do any good, she told herself sternly.
The important thing was to get
Fredbear out, before the water
soaked into his fur and made him
sink. But how was she going to do
that, when she couldn't even swim?

Pausing only long enough to give
Ian a kick on the shin, Ursula
hurried down from the bridge and

began to run along the river bank.

"Ursula! Come back!" shouted Ian, waving his arms and looking worried.

Ursula took no notice. She had just spotted Fredbear, in his bright yellow jumper, being swept around a bend in the river. She must keep him

in sight, or he would be lost for ever.

On and on ran Ursula, and soon she had left the town behind. The river began to wind its way through fields and woods, and there was nobody about except a few fishermen. The stream was wider here, and not so fast. Ursula was able to slow down to a walk, and still keep Fredbear's bobbing yellow jumper in view. Now was her chance.

She looked around to make sure

she was quite alone.

"I know *I* can't swim," said
Ursula. "But Ursula Bear can!" And
without wasting any more time she
pulled off her rucksack, unpacked the
currant bun and took a bite.

"I'M A BEAR, I'M A BEAR, I'M
A BEAR," chanted Ursula, chewing
the bun as she hurried along. "I'M A
BEAR, I'M A BEAR, I'M A
BEAR."

A few minutes later, Ursula had disappeared, and a small brown bear was scampering along the river bank on furry feet. The magic had worked, and once again she had turned into Ursula Bear.

Fredbear's yellow jumper was looking dangerously low in the water.

Ursula flung the rucksack into some bushes and dived into the river, making a splash which set all the ducks quacking in alarm. She swam strongly out into the stream, and soon she had a paw firmly round Fredbear's soggy middle.

Turning towards the bank, Ursula struggled to get Fredbear back to land. But the river was getting narrow again, the water swept her along, and a loud roaring noise filled her ears.

Suddenly she saw a big red-painted notice sticking up out of the water.

"What's a weir, Fredbear?" she said. Fredbear either didn't know, or his mouth was too full of water to reply.

It wasn't long before they both found out.

Chapter Four

Ursula clung to Fredbear with all her might as they went tumbling together over the edge of the weir. The sky vanished, the world went black, water filled her eyes and her ears, and for a long time she didn't know which way was up and which was down.

At last she was swept into calmer water, and found to her relief that she still had Fredbear clutched in her paws. She took a great gulp of air, glad to see blue sky again, and set off to swim for the shore.

Ursula was only a little way from the bank when she felt someone grab her by the shoulders, lift her out of the water, and set her on her feet on the grass. She stood there, dripping and staring, with Fredbear in her arms.

Her rescuer was a fisherman, wearing long green wellies past his knees and an old red jumper with holes in the elbows. He was staring at Ursula just as hard as she was staring at him.

"Good grief!" he said. "I don't believe this. A bear with a teddy? I'm seeing things!" Without waiting to pack up his fishing gear or his picnic basket, he turned and hurried away, muttering something about too much elderberry wine and sitting in the sun too long.

Ursula put Fredbear down in a patch of sunshine to dry. She was very glad that he was safe, but now she had a new problem. She had to

turn herself back into a girl again before she could go home, and there was no hope of finding beefburgers and chips on the river bank so far from the town.

She looked at the fisherman's lunch basket. There might be something in there which would do instead.

Ursula had to act quickly, for she knew the fisherman would be back before long.

"Sorry, fisherman," she said. "I wouldn't do this if I didn't have to." Then she opened the basket and put the contents one by one on the grass.

A bottle of home-made elderberry wine. A packet of sandwiches filled with something yellow and green that looked like mouldy cheese and smelled like it, too. A pork pie. Some chocolate biscuits. Another bottle of elderberry wine. Then, just as she was about to give up hope, she found something round wrapped in a plastic bag. It was a large bun, with sesame seeds on the top, and a big fat beefburger inside.

"Fredbear, look!" growled Ursula, jumping up and waving the beefburger in her paw.

Fredbear stared at the sky and said nothing. He didn't seem impressed at all.

Ursula sat down again with a bump. Fredbear was right. What was the use of a beefburger, without any chips?

Chapter Five

Carrying Fredbear and the
beefburger, Ursula trotted back
towards the town. It was nearly
lunch-time and the chip shop would
be open by now. Somehow she would
have to beg or steal a handful of
chips. Ursula didn't yet know how,
but she would worry about that
when she got there.

She hadn't gone very far when she
saw two girls coming towards her
along the bank and she scurried

quickly behind a tree until they had gone past. Then, as they came closer, Ursula stared hard at something they had in their hands. They were chatting and giggling as they walked along, and *eating chips out of paper bags with their fingers.*

"Chips!" said Ursula to herself. "What a bit of luck!" Then she dropped Fredbear and the beefburger and ran out from behind the tree. She scampered up to the girls and held up both her front paws.

"Please can I have some chips?" was what she meant to say, but in her growly bear's voice it didn't sound like that at all. All that came out was a fierce sort of "Grrrrrrr!"

The two girls almost jumped out of
their plimsolls in fright.

"Help! It's a bear!" cried one.

"It's going to bite us!" shouted the
other. They both flung their bags of
chips into the river and fled.

For the second time that day
Ursula had to go swimming, and
this time it wasn't to save Fredbear.
It was to rescue a couple of soggy
bags of chips which were rapidly
soaking up the water and beginning
to sink.

Ursula hurriedly dived in and
made a grab, but she was too late.

The ducks had beaten her to it. Quacking and squabbling and pecking at each other, they had torn the paper to shreds and gobbled up the chips before you could say tomato sauce.

"Greedy things!" said Ursula, as she climbed out onto the bank, empty-handed. Picking up Fredbear and the beefburger once more, she plodded off again towards the town, with water squelching out of her feet at every step.

She glanced about her as she went along, and after a while she recognised the place where she had dumped her rucksack. She poked about among the brambles, and there it was, safe and sound. It was only when she was pulling the strap onto her shoulder that she suddenly remembered what was in it. Egg and tomato sandwiches, orange juice, an apple, a carrot, and *a packet of smokey bacon crisps*.

Ursula opened the rucksack and stared at the crisps. "I wonder if they would work instead of chips," she said, turning them over in her paw. Crisps were only fried potatoes, after all. She decided it was worth a try.

Ursula hid among the brambles

and began to eat the beefburger and crisps, not forgetting to say the spell backwards as she munched.

"RAEB A M'I, RAEB A M'I, RAEB A M'I," she growled. "RAEB A M'I, RAEB A M'I, RAEB A M'I."

Two minutes later the little brown bear had vanished. The crisps had done the trick. Ursula was herself again, and feeling very pleased about it, too.

Chapter Six

The magic had worked just in time.
No sooner had Ursula set off for
home than she saw someone
hurrying anxiously towards her along
the bank. It was Aunt Prudence, still
in her apron and her old slippers,
and with her hair tumbling down
around her ears. Trailing along
behind her, looking shamefaced and
sorry for themselves, were Ian and
Jamie.

"Ursula! Thank goodness I've

found you!" cried Aunt Prudence when she saw her. "Are you all right?"

"I'm fine," said Ursula, hugging her aunt. Aunt Prudence plonked herself down on the grass to get her breath back.

"I couldn't make any sense of Ian's story," she puffed, mopping her hot face with her hanky. "Fredbear fell in the river . . . you ran off to try and save him . . . Ian and Jamie couldn't find you anywhere. At least they had the sense to come and fetch me."

Then Aunt Prudence noticed Fredbear, still in Ursula's arms and looking very damp.

"You've got Fredbear!" she said.

"However did you save him?" She stared at Ursula in horror. "I hope to goodness you didn't jump in!"

Ursula gazed at her aunt, thinking hard. She didn't want to tell fibs. On the other hand Aunt Prudence would never believe what really happened. She looked at her two cousins, who were staring at Fredbear in complete astonishment. They must never learn the true story, either.

"A fisherman got him out," she said at last. That was the truth, even though it wasn't quite the whole truth.

Aunt Prudence smiled, pleased that everything had turned out so well. She got up and brushed bits of grass from her apron.

"That was very kind of him," she said. "I hope you thanked him nicely, Ursula?"

Ursula remembered the fisherman waddling away in his wellies. She burst out laughing.

"I didn't get a chance to," she said. "He didn't seem to like bears much. Silly man!"

Ursula kissed Fredbear's damp nose and carried him off home before he caught a bad cold.